THE Selfish Giant

A TRADITIONAL STORY FROM EUROPE

Every day, the children came to play in the giant's garden.
It was a beautiful garden—a large garden with flowers
that danced and sparkled through soft, green grass
beneath the spreading fruit trees.

In the spring, the trees were covered in delicate blossoms
of pink, white, and pearl, and in the autumn,
they bore masses of rich, sweet fruit.

Birds flitted and twittered among the flowers and trees.
They sang so clearly and sweetly
that the children would stop in their play and listen.

"How happy we are," they said to each other.

One day, the giant returned.
He had been to visit his friend the Cornish giant
and had stayed away for seven years.
Now it was time to return to his own castle.

When he arrived, he saw the children playing in the garden.
"What are you doing in my garden?" he roared,
and the children ran away.
"My own garden is my own garden," he shouted,
"and nobody will play in it but me."

So he built a high wall all around it and put up notices.

He was a very selfish giant.

Now the children
had nowhere to play.

They would wander
around the high walls
of the giant's garden,
peeking through the cracks
and talking about
the beautiful garden they loved.

"How happy we were,"
they said to each other.

Then the spring came, and all over the country,
new flowers sparkled and danced through the soft, green grass.
Fruit trees covered themselves with blossoms,
and little birds twittered and sang in their branches.

But inside the walls, in the garden of the selfish giant,
the spring didn't come at all. It was still winter.
The soft, green grass stayed covered with snow,
and the trees stood silent and silver with frost.

Without the children's laughter, the birds didn't come,
the flowers stayed sleeping beneath the ground,
and the trees forgot to blossom.

The snow and the frost were happy.
"Spring has forgotten this garden," they cried,
"so we will live here all the year around."

They asked the north wind to come and stay.
He came wrapped in furs, and he roared all day and all night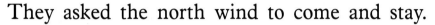
around the garden.
"This is a wonderful place," he said.
"We must ask the hail to come and stay."

The hail came all dressed in pearls with her breath as cold as ice.
She rattled and crashed on the roof of the castle
and ran around and around the garden as fast as she could.

The selfish giant was puzzled.
"I cannot understand why the spring hasn't come,"
he said to himself.

But the spring didn't come, and nor did the summer.
All over the country, the autumn gave red and golden fruit
to the trees in every garden, but the trees in the
selfish giant's garden were left covered with frost and snow.
"He is too selfish," the autumn said.

So it was always winter in the giant's garden, and the snow,
the frost, the north wind, and the hail were happy there.

One morning, the selfish giant was wakened
by a new and beautiful sound.
It was such sweet and lovely music that he thought
the King's musicians were passing by.

It was only a little bird singing outside his window.
He had not heard the sound of birds singing for so long,
it seemed to him like the most beautiful music
in the whole world.

Then he noticed that the north wind and the hail were quiet,
and the air was filled with a soft and sweet perfume.

He saw the most wonderful sight.
The children had crept in through a hole in the wall
and were sitting in the branches of every tree that he could see.

The trees were so happy to have the children back again
that they had covered themselves with blossoms of pink,
white, and pearl.
The birds flitted and twittered happily in and out of the branches,
and the flowers danced and sparkled through the soft, green grass.

As the selfish giant stood watching, he saw that spring had come to all but one corner of the garden.

In that one corner it was still winter, and standing there, all alone, was a little boy.

He was so small that he could not reach up to the lowest branches of the tree, and he was crying bitterly.

The tree stood covered with frost and snow, and the north wind roared and blew around it.

The tree bent its branches down as low as it could in the wind and said, "Climb up. Climb up, little boy."

The little boy tried and he tried, but he was too tiny to reach them.

The selfish giant's heart melted.
"How selfish I've been," he said.
"Now I know why the the spring didn't come."

When the children saw the selfish giant
come out of the castle into the garden,
they were very frightened and ran away.

The garden became winter again.

Only the little boy didn't run.
He was crying so hard
that he didn't see the selfish giant coming.
Very gently, the selfish giant took the little boy
and placed him safely on the branch of the tree.

At once, the tree covered itself with blossoms,
and the birds came to twitter and sing.
The little boy was happy. He reached out
and put his arms around the giant's neck
and kissed him on the cheek.

When the other children saw
that the giant was gentle and kind,
they came running back into the garden.
With them came the spring again.

"It is your garden now,
little children," said the giant,
and he took down the signs and knocked down the walls.

From that day on, the children played in the giant's beautiful garden.

And the selfish giant was never selfish again.